ROADMAP HANDS

MARJORIE A. THOMAS

Print ISBN: 978-1-7347946-0-1

eBook ISBN: 978-1-7347946-1-8

Cover Design and Illustration by Marjorie A. Thomas

www.marjorieathomas.com

Printed in the United States of America

First Edition

For Lewand.

You are the most beautiful and unexpected surprise of my life. Thank you for finding me.

To playing the game, by your side, always.

For that.

ACKNOWLEDGMENTS

This book would not have been finished today,
without the support, and inspiration of a handful of
very important people. While they may not have been
with me during the writing process, with all of their
strong influence, they very well may have.

Thank you Mom and Dad, for your limitless support,
fierce love, and never-ending encouragements
to pursue my passions, in spite of obstacles.

Thank you to my dear friend, Jamie Bolander, for being
a constant source of insight, wisdom, and for our ever
reflective, beautiful conversations, after which I always
seem to walk away with something new.

Thank you Bryan Fuller for the creation of *Pushing Daisies*,
greatest television show I have ever witnessed to this day,
which has to some degree definitely fueled my curious
obsession with exploring death through artistic lenses—
but, you know, in a fun way. Of course.

Thank you also to my eighth grade english teacher, Mrs.
Williams, for that first A+ on my first poetry "book."
Bound inside a plastic binder and strewn with colored
pencil illustrations. You were there at the sparking
of a lifelong passion. Thank you all.

CONTENTS

<u>Somewhere Along the Way</u>:

And in the Going:

ROADMAP HANDS

In The Beginning:

The Stork, He Wants to Know

Swollen prego belly
heave-ho'
heave-ho'
push forth holy baby.

Grow, grow, *grow*
into the expectations,
pre-considerations
make up little ones.

Amalgamation brain,
but sim'lar buns
to the rest of us.

Soon as air's familiar
with your lungs
it's time to run,
to *run* away from labels.

Notions, stereotype lotions,
enticing, snake-oil potion
tricksters swear'll fix ya' like
the addict sun grew used to
living as the spotlight did.

Moon comparatively
nothing more than dust
and dead old footprints.

Tell me now, little one,
while you've still got the time,
still got a say to keep on
keepin' on this way.

You wanna come,
you wanna join?

This sound like fun?
I'll wait, but know
just know, that if
the answer's yes,
you know, oh little one,

I'm sorry but
you've gotta fight.

Play the Game

You are a child.
Moon-faced you
with the tooth-
in-tongue-
in-cheek-
in-tently eyed smile.
You make me better
than I would have been
for never having
known you.

No please, don't give me that
grimace-lipped
puckered-face
dis-prop-ortionate smile.
Curls shaking with every side-to-side,
every turning of the head.
Strongly opposed to pedestal-like heights,
you are,
and yes,
I know this.

Trust, that this
does not make
you any bigger than
you need be.
Not in this head, at least.
Can we be children on
the playground, please?
Curious bees.
The two of us, bright,
buzzing questions marks.

We'll dive wildly,
belly-flopping.

Spread-eagling for the answers,
like on a slip n' slide.

Water flowing down our neon river bed.
On backyard grass patch,
plastic-
caught-
between-
our-ass-cheeks kind of days.
Promise to remind me, *live*.
Okay?
Lace your fingers in mine,
and I'll do the same.

Sing me your unspoken dreams.
I'll echo in refrain.

Read me the lines you know
will pull me down
to the Earth again.
Play the game, with me, okay?
Cos' love, we're only children.
Jumping at the chance to build ourselves
one-hell-of-an-
im-per-man-ent legacy.
Play the game with me.
Okay?

Exhibition

You stand there with your nose pressed
nearly flat up against the glass.
Protecting little detailed charcoal squiggles,
and smiling smally to yourself.
Although the piece was drawn by
hands which moved, which drew
long before you and your time
you feel as if the inspiration—
feel just like those flying, rapturous
creative sparks it gives you
is something you were meant
to stumble on.
As if it's been sitting there patiently
waiting especially for you.
You, special you.
Tucking tiny inspiration doodles
into your breast pocket.
You pat happily, your shiny new
love to return to.

Shapes

We shape ourselves
into what we think
the world wants us to be.

We change ourselves
inside and out
to what is accepted in society.

It takes years to be able,
to bury the things
we wish to hide from one another;

and a lifetime to uncover
the parts of ourselves
we never should have let go.

<u>Cosmic Beauty</u>

If she were the Moon
I'd be the stars.
Suspended in the open space,
like little golden lanterns.
Floating in a lazy race
towards the heavens,
and in their Godlike magnificence
I would make little haste
in deciding that your beauty is
the driving force behind
the universe's expansion.
For only so much loveliness and grace
could be contained within a single galaxy.
Let alone an infinite amount.

Origin

To you, paradise prison cell.
Unbounded beauty beats against
the white of your stone walls.
One giant heartbeat.
I press my palm into the sand.
Warm, smooth, un-corrosive grains.
I feel why people love you.

From this cell I can see
the beauty of a country,
woven in the fabric of my clothes.
My reality rags.
Dressed in the body of a king,
my skin reflects the love of this holy sun.

Brown me, kiss me please, on the cheek.
Unlike a lover.
I am but one small piece of your puzzle.
Provide me food, and peace,
and I am happy to stay here with you.
Just so long as these bars hold,
and my back can rest itself against its window.

In the morning I am caught
between the crossfire of dawn
and these ancient crumbling fortress walls.
Rise up, *rise up!* Remember to take care.
Take care to not let night fall, not here, because
sometimes the shadows are more than just that.

Fruit Bearing Tree

Take a hulking bite out of the honey, sweet.
So small, in my palm,
yet I feel it's juices running down my cheek,
all the way down to my dogged feet.
The wind blows calm
so calmly that if I turned and
puffed myself up
spit my seeds out to the wind
they would return to me.
"Perhaps they'll plant themselves,"
I think and throw the core down below
tumbling softly into bleak and nothing.
Perhaps I'd feel like a G-O-D
if I had such a complex.
Spitting life just to see where it lands.
Perhaps I don't care what the end result is.
When I'm sated I'll just walk away,
and that's it.
Perhaps lonely seeds pray to
a sun that they can't see.
Perhaps we just happen to be
the spitballs that stick.

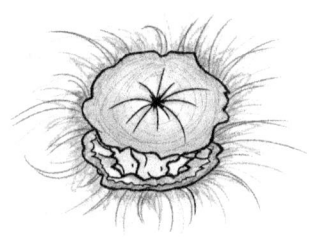

Intimate Insight Between Mother & Child

She holds her hand out.

Strong, lofty woman with the
tender eyes.

Fingers spread, spaces in-between
for the little, little one's to fit.
They fold together, and begin the chant
without breaking eye contact.

Softly she says
to her anxiety riddled child,
"We are now, we are now, we are now."

The child stops her crying,
stuffs the dry heaves down,
with the tears that stop there.
Between her somber-bellied hiccup breaths
she wavers softly,
"we are now, we are now, we are now."

Together they repeat the words,
until the child has calmed down,
and she's on the ground again.

What Lives Behind Their Eyes?

What lives behind their eyes?
In pools of deep blues and shallow greens?
Or darker tones in black disguise,
and some which fall at in-betweens.

What lives behind their eyes?
From burning memories to bitter ashes;
but each recollection with its purpose,
forms a lifetime wreathed in lashes.

What battles have been lost by he,
who averts his gaze as the world brushes by?
A man whose eyes much like a sea,
hold secrets pulled in with the tide.

What hopes and dreams are kept by she,
who still is young and without heartache?
This little girl who cannot yet see,
the precious joys that life can take.

What lives behind their eyes?
For each of us the story ranges.
Enough so that we sympathize,
with saddened looks and soft exchanges.

Soundly

The shift between the world
of wakefulness and sleep
is deadly fast and dark.
Between the closing of heavy eyes
and the shutting down of busy minds
there is a quiet force which creeps
on silent soles.
Searching for the very end
of where your faded conscience roams.

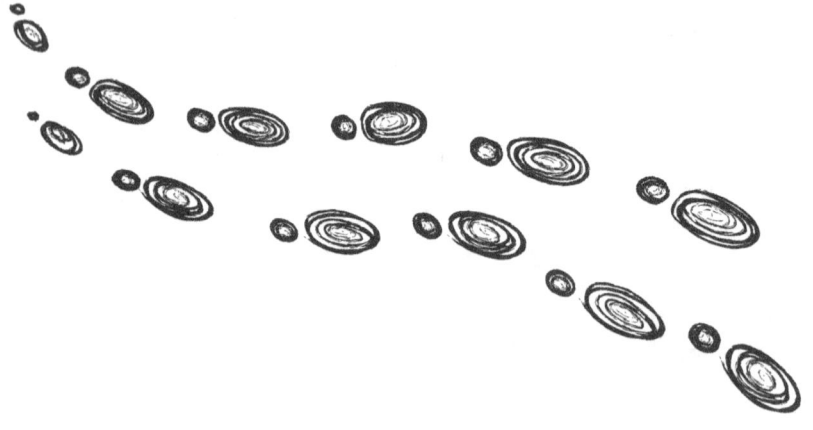

Footprints

The earth is cold and it is gray.

I take this as a sign that you are okay.

You said you always felt your very best
when the air outside was sharp enough
to pierce your tongue,
yet kind enough so as to untangle your hair
for you.

The hair you never brushed.

Had I not known you for your
neatly-trimmed behavior,
I would expect multitudes of tiny leaves,
just growing from your roots,
caught in the ringlets that had
always looked more at home in nature,
rather than pulled back tight into
a rope against your neck.

The breath you drew had always felt
from my eyes to expel itself with purpose.

As if your lungs knew that each inhale was
a gift, not a given.
Knowing that each one may have well
been your last,

you learned to make them count.
You learned to note the time, but forwent
meaning the numbers of all else.

How many years you collected seemed
to matter very little.

Tracking your footprints, wiling,
winding down a frozen way
I gather that your straying is purposeful.
Felled by unencumbered love and trust,
but where you've gone now I can't say.
Firmly rooted, I hold true that downfalls could be
so much worse than this fate.

To vanish quite completely, without even
the slightest trace of a footprint in your place.

Center of Your Own

Bubble gum thoughts.
Shoe-string lies.
Untie your own logic,
and chew reality,
carefully.
Be mindful, mindful
of the way it slithers down
your boa constrictor throat.
Stomach moat,
gut churning with this idea of
cosmic-level uncertainty.
You will never know which
corner of the universe you came from.
Or understand
that the system inside you
is as much in decay
as the solar one surrounding you.
Expanding with each breath.
Beautiful.
Incomprehensible.
Bound for collapse.

Observations 4:18

Surfer in the granite wind.
Icy. Oblong. Blind—
among other unrelated words
which come to mind.
Also, fucking cold.

Baseball-cap-man and dog, walk.
Paw print after print,
imprinted in sand.
Unending glory canopy above my head
shifts in variations of slate
blue-white and pink.

Where I fit in feels like a faded memory.
Watching as surfer leaps above
the deathly crest of a wave,
only to disappear
again, again, again.
Board and all.

Just bored is all.
That's all these observations are.

Like a Picture on a Metal Plate

Dancing eyes burn holes inside
an open white reflection, blank
malignant heart pain, pinkened sky veins,
null below the growing of
another dying dusk.

The sun was tired today.
He was burnt out of heat and flames.
Epic glow ran thin across these pastel walls.

Gigantic, upright, slant accounts for
grand, illusive size.
Outfitted by countless, bare-bones,
square windows.
Doors shut around the other fading people.

Yesterday seemed brighter, didn't it?
Often times, no one answers my questions.
Undermining the soul which cradles bone
around your pumping,
racing, radi-cally lame life vessel.

Heart has not a clue of what to say.
Every beat excruciat-ing-ly slow.
Aching takes its toll, and so they're told to
reach their palms pressed flat together now
turn inwardly, rip open, and make room for me.

<u>Naivety</u>

She diverged quite suddenly from the path
which she herself had set upon.
Out of want or need for spontaneity.
Or for stupidity,
and how little credit she gave to her own;
she wandered off into the dark
and un-braved wood.

She told herself repeatedly that no one else
would dare wander as far as she
from road, from safety, certainty.
Despite the trodden ground before her,
she brushed blithely past the broken,
bended leaves.

To feel special was needed,
was so desired by her delicate
and unforgiving psyche.

"I need to be lost as no one has before.
I need to find my way out without aid, without
reliance on a single soul except my own."

"Only then will I have proven once and for all
that it is quite within the realm of *possible*
to need absolutely nobody at all."

As of today, no body is to be found, up and down
and all throughout those callow woods.

Art of Knowing Nothing

Oh, if I could only
pretend myself to be anyone
but this, I would be
anything else, but who I am today.

I feel that there has been
too little growth,
given such ample time,
and too many lines crossed,
into dangerous hills
with judgmental eyes;
and after all of these
barefaced, naked,
white-knuckled lies,
I have come to surmise
that the first real jump,
the true test of my guise,
is the honest acceptance
that deep down inside

I know nothing.

I know nothing
save the beat of my own heart;
soft and steady,
like footsteps in time with the rain.
Nothing but
the cold air in my lungs
drawing life from the people around me;
the lovely,
unbreakable ones.
So while,
I may know next to nothing, except
the slash of a pen,
or the slicing of wounds with a brush,
when I bleed there is no red.

I flow in every color.

Much like art.

Somewhere Along the Way:

Observations 12:5

I sip the warm sickly sweet
savoring the warm coating effect on my throat.
Curled up hands and cup
eyes peer over the rim smeared with a gentle lip stain.
Quietly I watch the people.
There is man with bagel,
cream cheese and a mid-yawn face.
Breath heavy and laborious
between bite and bite and bite.
"Spare change miss'please?"
Finger stubs poke out of gloves below my chin
I look down with chagrin because already
I have sped ten paces farther'head.
It is cold today.
Crowd of youngsters with their heads bent
fixedly over the now drugs of their choice.
Who would choose human interaction
over the intermittent dopamine hits
of stranger's approval, far away?
Quick-pace, quick-pace, quick-pace,
caught among the somber throng of
blue collars and shivering people.
What is the purpose of all your hurry?
Where on your way must be so damn important
that you push and you groan and bemoan
inconvenience sent
straight from the heavens to your king of
king of dead end doorsteps?

Where?

Morning Service

Those fingernails are long and filthy.
Crusted with blood.
Black shitty nail beds
reaching for two slices of
whole-grain unbuttered toast.
Man tips his head and nods,
hair still drippin' from the flood outside.
"You'd think Noah was calling again,"
he says.
Spit flying from the mouth,
without a sound
making his rounds.
Sweet smile without a host.
Green eyes that peer outwardly,
good, real nice, real swell.
Even grinnin—
grimac—
grinning, but somehow,
still looking quite lost
without a home,
without a boat,
with little hope,
of keepin' the current down.

He's an Artist Man

That boy's an artist.
Troubled, poor thing.
Weeping weak alkaline drops of
watered-down coffee beans.
Caffeine's the only drug
he's got the stomach for.
Though poets score more
women doing harder stuff.
Tough luck's your gasoline.
Guzzle down drops of sympathy.
Petty rain spots on black concrete.
Your belly only doesn't eat itself
by the kindness of scraps
from strangers though.
This is romantic, no?
That boy's an artist.
Walking elegy
for the creatures that he
swears himself to be.
Only one clued onto
Keats, Rivera, Burroughs,
Whitman, less so Kahlo, shame.
Please, you know, you should
only be so blessed to be
counted in esteem
among these.
Self-proclaimed artist,
tortured artist.
Sure thing, man.

Deadbeat Sweets

Feed me in
poetry.

I want not for empty calories.
In reams of crisp and honeyed couplets
speak to me!

Slabs of calorie dense sheets,
faded and marked by ravenous hands
who feast upon their bloodied meat
like wild dogs in Guanajuato's heat.

The body minds itself, but I forget to eat.
More often satiated by long lines of
Rimbaud, Smith and Keats—yet somehow,
I am left feeling as though I have
succumbed to gluttony.

As if flower blossoms of sugar and fat
adorned my wasted insides, wanting more than
wine and ink, drunk off of pages that perpetuate
their wisdom—birthed equally, by vanity
and misery.

Full to bursting with it—shit—
picking your teeth
with so many sharpened exclamations,
salty sacchariney statements,
words that tried to make a point.

Bloody. Rebellious.
So damnably lovely.

Deadbeat sweets.
Delight in these
deadbeat sweets.

Enlightened, these
deadbeat sweets.
Filling me to the brim.

Toothache

She winces in pain.
Hand shooting up to hold
the tender meat of her jaw,
which feels now on the verge of
bursting outward, raw.

Where wisdom teeth
may have grown once,
instead a pair of hands
and squinting yellow eyes
claw themselves forward from
the back of her throat.

Everything she had once thought
ugly and banished
from herself by force
so many years before
comes tearing back up
lit by great fire and urgency.

"You cannot force the demons down,"
she thought, choking on gobs
of wishful thoughts.

To ever think she could escape
had been her first mistake.

The second was forgetting that
they had existed in the first place.

Thirdly, tragic, foolish, hoping,
and denying that they might ever return to her.

"You are not better than your demons,"
they say; "for all their seeming absence
they still live inside you, to this day."

Nodding, she garbles almost-words,
but knows not what to do.
Except but rub her bleeding gums
biting her tongue, and worsely
opening the cavity, anew.

Kaifuku

私はとても喜んで私の唯一の家族の愛を受けた胃を開始しました
(I've starved the stomach that so gladly received the love
of my one and only family)

自己主義的に自分の自己破壊に出席するためにそれらを離れてプッシュ
(pushing them away to selfishly attend to my own self-
destruction)

私が認めるのは
(which I admit was going well)

あなたが来るまで
(until you came along)

そして私は再び永遠の暗闇の中で希望を見つけました
(and I once again found hope in the perpetual darkness)

自分の静かな存在の
(of my own quiet existence).

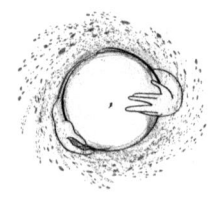

City of Fog (v. 1)

We first met
on the outskirts of a city
that neither of us had
had the chance
to call home
just yet.

Do you remember?
Do you remember
the night I let my heart
beat itself a lullaby
into the curvature
of your spine
for the very first time?

Back then
I thought you must be
the most beautiful boy
that I had ever seen.
Even today, I have yet
to prove otherwise.

Your lips
did not kiss lightly.
No, not like the way
the early morning fog
clings oh so
lovingly, to the shore,
but more along the lines,

of a beggar in the Tenderloin
left out to brace the freezing cold.

<u>Expectations</u>

Even the softest silk
may
chafe

against your
coarse
sandpaper skin

and flies will take
their drink in
blood and honey,

taking no preference in
which one
you decide to spill

and where the sun
may be as quick
to burn you

to a crisp
just as it is
to warm your freezing bones

you will give in and lie low
sighing burgeoningly slow
open-kneed and gritted teeth

unsatisfied with living
and your heavy eyes just
waiting for that dawn beyond the peak

hard halfway heart knowing
it never happens like this
sloughed off love and desolation

trail growing behind you
wise to look back only if for a moment
assess what damage you've done and press on?

Confused & Laying Down

Dream about his thighs
wishing that you might find
excitement in them.
Ecstasy in rough fingertips
and short pricks, drawing
hot, unspoken blood between
the two of you.
Conceding yours in his;
yet, he does nothing with it;
and so you try and try again
with other men,
in different beds,
with different names
but every body feels the same.
Is the problem
you or them?
This how it was supposed to be?
Are they unhappy just as you?
Scared and confused
that they should be
with some body else?
Ashamed, conflicted,
dreaming of alternatives.
A familiar kind of love
might ease the pain
bit by little bit.
The question is
what if you're wrong,
and this is it?

Unexpected Attraction

Perverse thoughts, in the way of
pursed lips
and swung hips
and the way you would sway,
and smile,
and nod in my direction.
Giving me my first sense of how
it felt to be truly attracted to someone.
As if the magnetic poles
between our chests
existed solely
to bring us closer together—
breath by breath,
mouth on neck—
your delicate hands making quick work
of the clasp that holds
both halves of me together.
You remember
to undress me with precaution
because you know that
each step farther you get
I might just run and hide again.
This you might
just understand
better than anyone
that I've met yet.

Night Terrors

The phantom sensation of
fingers tickling
the back of her throat
causes her stomach to clench
painfully in reflex.
She is less stirred from waking
than tossed roughly from the sea of dreams—
she now realizes is just a tangle of limp
and sweaty bed sheets.
Wrapped tight and strangling around
her twisting body,
she needs to get them O-F-F,
and forcefully caterpillars herself
in order to be freed
of this unintentional cocoon.
"Dreams will make themselves true
if you let them"
a small voice inside her brain crows,
reminding her of this unmeaning
tendency she seems to have.
To act out dreams in real life,
if they weighed heavy enough on her mind.
This involved movement most of the time,
and sometimes speech,
in the same way
that a dog will twitch and whine
during fits of unrestful sleep.

Less piss in the bed sheets though.

Lie with Me

You always seemed to have
the hardest time
when it came to sleeping.
You would close your eyes
and grind your teeth
like you were trying to make meal
out of the bone dust,
and sometimes
I would catch a lonely tear
which had dripped down
the side of your face
into my hair,
and I was scared
that maybe you already knew
what I had hiding in there.
Believe me,
I can keep secrets for a long time;
but at some point
the close-lipped lies
become loud enough, wild enough
to shake the bed
and wake up all the people
outside.
So please, sleep still darling.
No one needs to know
what goes on underneath
our bedsheets.

<u>What I'd Do for a F*cking Eraser</u>

I can rip out as many pages as I'd like.
I can tear you from my life just out of spite.
I can cross you, slash you, write out
of stories that were all about
the two of us
and maybe now

I'll go back to writing everything in pencil.

See Me, See Me

See me,
I want to cry
out, waiting, hoping
any passerby might turn and look,
might really look and
see me, see me!
I cry out, loud enough to drown
the ebb and flow of voices
growing faint beneath my own.
They rise and fall
much like the murmuring of distant waves;
so very constant, so assuredly there
that even I can't hear them anymore.
See me, see me!
I cry and receive no love.
No sympathy from anyone.
I am blind, and scared
and losing hope that I might be the only one.
See me, see me!
I cry, for I am only just
a creature born of aimlessness and fear.
So panicked, and so awfully unaware
that were I to simply reach
my trembling hands out
maybe, maybe I might see you there.
Equally blind,
equally thrust in complete darkness
stumbling about.

You, Uncomfortable Reminder

You are holding the scraps of somebody's
broken life in your hands,
and all you can see looking down
are the fissures of tale-telling age lines.
The cracks of your own palms.

You are reminded of mortality.
Taking away from these leftover pieces
nothing of their significance.
It does not matter what or who they were.
You imagine that even Death might be
of half a mind to call you selfish.
"I am not here for you yet," he hisses,
prickling the light hairs
on the back of your neck.

"It is of no use wasting time worrying when
or where we'll meet again,
I can assure I will be back."
Says you: nothing.
You are looking down at your hands
and at those broken pieces.
Crying not for them but for
the reminder that they serve to you.
"One day, I will be nothing but broken pieces."

One day no more than this.

Fragments of a life half-lived.
Never will I come close,
to accomplishing my all.

There is not enough time.
Simply not enough time.

Do not make me think about this any more.

Into the Water

Frightened fingers fumbling
inside heavy coat pockets.
Where the lining is hardly
but enough to keep away
the cold. Oh, the cold,
how it must love so much
that shivering frame of yours
At least more than sunlight does.
What other reason would it have
to make its home inside such
shaky bones? Nothing else left
but guts and smoke. You take
another drag from the last
cigarette you own, and toss
the smoldering ashes in the sand.
Your shoes are wet, the water
wraps itself around your ankles,
filled with salt and piss
and hunger. You are thankful
for the rocks inside your
heavy, thin coat pockets.
Perhaps they might make it easier
for you to let go of the breath
that you always seemed to live for;
and yet never lost the sense
that each inhale felt much the same
as both lungs filling up with water.

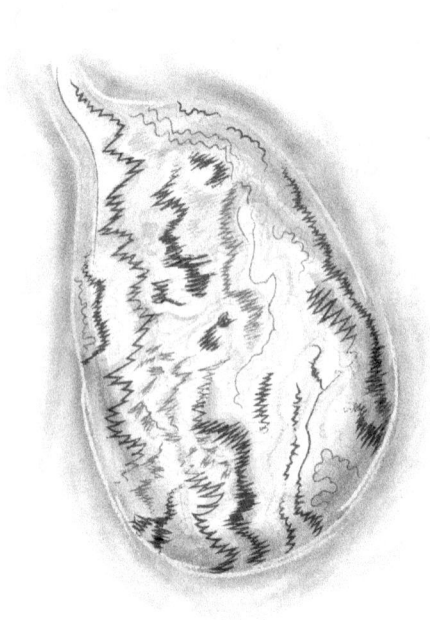

<u>Gone</u>

How many times do I have to look up
before I stop expecting to see you?
Sitting in the empty space across from me,
maybe smiling.
Maybe examining the undersides
of your fingernails, alternating chewing
between lip and cheek in that way
you used to do.
Maybe you are looking away, staring off,
into the space behind my head
because it feels better, maybe, than
ungrounding in my eyes.
Maybe yours bore into me,
almost as indifferently they would
taking in some
hack job, tasteless, painting.
Maybe your own listless reflection.
Maybe all of these things.
Maybe none.

Most likely none.

And in the Going:

The Journey Home

Let me fly in the way
it seems you,
as a bird,
would.

Short, fluttering pumps, sporadic
palpitations.
Just enough to know that
wings will carry you,
and that your light, hollow-boned skeleton
is best fitted for the sky.

Trust that each pause,
trust that every drop in altitude
inches you not towards the flat
unwelcome palm of ground;
but rather like a rest stop,
teaches you that there is strength
in not flying forever.

Delicate, beautiful, mountainous folds.
Valley fabric in it's highs and lows.
Sun-kissed, raining, misted thick
in cloud shadows.

Suburban streets wind themselves.
Box cars and train wheels,
on and off again from beaten tracks.
From this dizzyingly high up
home looks differently, a little differently.

Home is little ant houses,
roofs over little ant people,
living little and lives, inside
their concrete doll-drum metropolis.

So you nestle in your slice of sky
with eyes drawn up for life
and heart cast down to beat itself
to loved ones down below at all times.

Check the Pockets

Unfold these.
Read me.
Understand my center is
the same as where yours came from.
That heart inside you is the only one
I'll ever find this way.
Loathe to tear away,
yet searching for the next checkpoint already.
Infinite, sheltering tree.
Busy cafe, empty but for us.
Tangled white sheets.
Departure gate.
Forget goodbyes.
See you again love.
In our separate
alternate pocket timeline.

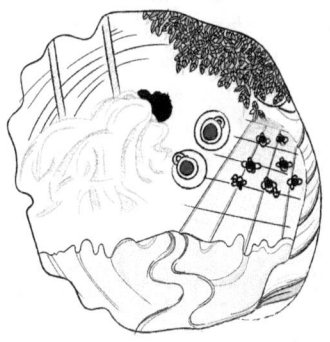

Youth

Catch myself at times.
Thinking about
the child I once was.
I must have been.
Catch myself poring over dregs.
Leftovers of my gawkiness;
such as the carriage of my body.
Reminding me subtly in
the gentle rotund curve
of my ever-present toddler belly.
The natural "pooch" of all youth.
Except for that they never care
to suck their guts in
like I do.
Oh, this body that was once six,
and seven,
and eight,
and zero point nine-nine.
This clock o' mine
started ticking soon as I had grown
the right number of ventricles.
Those pink and squishy chambers
pumping blood into my baby-bone fingers,
into the capillaries of my one brown eye.
Came into this world squinting, I did.
I've shed my skin now
more times than I could ever hope to count;
but miraculously have always had
the same amount of ribs.
The same pertinacious heart.
This time around,
mostly been called by two names.
Mine and yours.
Like to assign / ume don't you?
Think you know me.
Do you?

"YOU" everyone collective.
Handing me a sticky label,
asking me to paste it to my white chest.
Spelling out "HI, MY NAME IS . . ."
but ah, oh precious you,
I know well enough by now who I am.
Who I've become.
Might've come out squinting yes,
but you see?
It just so happens that
the other eye is open now.

Photographs

There are some things that a photograph
just cannot capture.
Like the feeling of a cold breeze,
whispering against my cheek;
the setting sun at my back,
much like an encouraging pair of warm hands,
pushing me gently forward, into the arms
of the welcoming sea.

Praise be! For all machinery that
may so effortlessly capture beauty,
in neatly packaged squares of tangibility.
Such an intriguing and tempestuous notion,
to simply have to point, and click, and *flash!*
That moment then in part
becomes your own to keep.
I assure you still, that I can see,
just as well, using the lenses that G-d gave me.

And even if an image truly met its worth,
fully expressed, yet still contained
within 1,000 words,
it begs the question, why?
Now, why would anybody take the time?
Attempting to describe the way
those stars that wink and flicker
on the verge of every night
mirror so loyally the skyline
to the city I was born.

Such life beguiles me, tucked away
inside the margins of cheap postcards.
From strange lands that boast
great distance from my home
and all its grave familiarity.
Dreaming to take care that no matter where I go

the sun and sea are plentiful,
the words are bursting full of flavor,
the people treasure more than paper,
and the love there is more than enough
to keep my belly full.

City of Fog (v. 2)

We first met
on the outskirts of a city
that neither of us had
had the chance
to call home just yet.

Do you remember?
Do you remember
the night I let my heart
beat itself a lullaby
into the curvature
of your spine
for the very first time?

Back then it seemed
I might have had
the stomach for more lies.
Feeding myself in spoonfuls
of a half-love
I was convinced I should be grateful for.
After all, some people starve.

"These lips do not kiss lightly,"
I thought.
No, not like the way
the early morning fog
clings oh so
lovingly, to the shore,
but more along the lines

of a beggar in the Tenderloin
left out to brace the freezing cold.

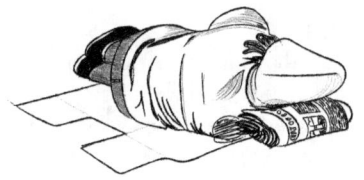

I Remember Your Face

There was a time.
May have been a time
where steep concrete hills
would have not been combated
in heels, but rather in
flashing pink sneakers.

My size 3's, chasing feet
which at the time were still
nearly twice as big as mine.
So young, and so quick to believe
you might always slow down for me.

Your face is older now.
It takes a second but to recognize,
from far away
approaching slowly, click by click,
your eyes look up, and it seems as if
after all these years you still can feel me coming.

We start out slowly,
two polar ice caps thawing, exchanging niceties,
and we talk, and we talk, and we talk,
and I think, *"how strange,"* to myself.
Feels strange to be well,
spiteful of little things.

Plucking at worn strings inside the casing
of a heart that used to play for yours.
I've been hearing little
whispers through the grapevine
that you've got a girl.
A woman, and she's fine.

When you say her name, I feel it.
That phantom aching.

Even after all this time.
After all the years we've passed on by
it almost feels worse, to know
that life moves on.
Even after a heartbreak
as painful as ours
how insane now to think
we survived.

<u>Shut Away</u>

Hiding myself away from the world.
Closing tightly the blinds,
so that no sunlight may slip
through the cracks.
Shutting quickly the door,
so that no one may see
what lies inside.
I do these things
and yet still hold up false hope
that someone may come along
and see that closed door
along the hallway expanse of
seven billion more,
loud, colorful, and invitingly warm,
and think maybe
to open this one.
Maybe learning what lies inside
could be something
worthwhile.
Maybe.

Maniac Jacket

I can feel the track that runs crazy, twisting,
tangling, winding wildly in my head.
Cassette tape veins,
black licorice, snake tongues,
scrambling rapid-fire neurons.
Their shapes all bend, all stretch
alongside the gravity motions of my skull.
Now shaking itself so as to
knock the grime out, dusty walls loose.
How am I supposed to navigate
my way through?
Eyes squeeze, tightly, tight-shut,
shuttered-but, wholly transparent.
From behind I can read the flow of blood
trickling down through tender-veined canals.
My body washed in red that glows,
a glowing red, a-glowing, glow.
I feel more a dollhouse skeleton,
jammed tightly into the doorframe,
than a real person anymore.
Unsure of who, or where, or what
of home is left for me to crawl back for.

Welcome, Unwanted Guest

The pain.
It comes and goes in waves.
In the back of my mind I can feel it throbbing,
pulsing, growing silently
like a cancerous tumor,
swelling rapidly to fit just barely
inside the confines
of my battered skull.
Oh, how I could so easily
peel back the skin
and find little bits of you inside,
scratching at the soft pink walls.
Tapping on the glass panes of my
fogged-up eyes
just waiting
for the storm to pass outside.

Even then, you never seem to leave.

<u>Anxieties</u>

Whispers of yellow burning
riddling the insides of your eardrums.
Golden like weeds baked by the sun;
unnerving in the plucking of.
Tickling cruelty of anxious thoughts
prick at your brain.
Needles lost in hay, needless to say
you're in the fucking thick of it.

"Present you've robbed me!"
you complain. "Joy's a joke!"
"How could you ask a smile
from the hopeless hoping sacks
who've learned to live without?"
Questions from indignant
man / woman / sancti-
monious maniac.

Where are you then?
How about where your head's at?
Might as well be detached
from the neck down for how far
your eyes've rolled back to the past.
Cut out those wires, that got you so hyper-
ecstatic to detach yourself from here and
from this here and now.

This here and now.

The Descent

Shaking limbs
ice-bone knees bracing
for that fatal wind
to knock me off my feet.
Tears stream and I commit
my brain to playing games
that safer make
me able to get
down and off
the mountain.

Afraid,
        afraid,
                afraid,

but I embrace the feeling.
Fragile heart pounds
and swells and splits open
and suddenly
out of the bloody seed
a flower grows.

Highland's Edge

Grey pallor on the lake
shining
in such a blue way.

Lights dance across pale yellow;
accompanying the animated flashes
of fluid tree branch fingers.

A fractured face in pieces, smiling;
and the sliver of your smiling
wondrous eye.

Watching curiously,
when able-bodies journey
across stretches of winding black road.

Twisting trees
scattered among rock and snow,
and blinding white like bone.

In this place, forgotten place, God,
the winds sing songs, and everything
bleeds far too deadly beautiful to take.

Roadmap Hands

I am old.

Mottled and bruised as a rotting peach.
Well past my prime.
My hands are not my hands.
For I know myself
to have quick and nimble fingers,
dressed delicate in soft pink flesh.
Hull-carcass, weather-beaten ones I've got now.

Blue veins bulging, like rivers drunk
just after heavy rains.
Scarred knuckles and dried nail beds,
so brittle now that twigs might suffer
pressure with more grace.
I listen for the great booming of Death
and every measured step he makes.
So close, so very confident,
and closing in the distance.

While it fills the air enough to make me
turn my head,
I feel the beat marching inside my chest.
Head down, eyes sharp, grazing the palms.
Neither smooth nor wrinkled.
Bone, just bone, that's it.
Skin shed, eyes wide, I am
more than shaken now,
to be nothing, save
this feeble skeleton.

That ceaseless march has trailed
off to silence now.
Heart still. I lift my quivering chin
to look up at his ageless face and gape.
He stoops down low to meet me with

a piercing gaze.
Eyes strange. Not like the windows of mine;
but mirrors, which reveal me now for
everything I am.

Was.

Small, wild-haired, and rosy-cheeked.
Two loose teeth and bloodied knees.
Small thing, tiny breasts, round growing hips.
Rejecting father, son, and holy spirit
in hot pursuit of some "original" belief.
Shrinking, sagging skin, and furrowed brows.
Crinkling eyes and roadmap hands.
All my years behind me now.

Having been patient,
he will wait no longer to collect me.

Offering me his gentle, boney hand,
I reach up shakily, and grab hold.
Without fear for where it is
that he might take me.
I am trusting as we walk together,
hand in hand, almost as if
lifelong friends.

"I've been waiting all this time for you,"
he hums, a sweet song, ancient, soft.
Suddenly then, the world transforms,
feeling to me like nothing but
the safest, purest, warmest love.

We hold, quiet, and still.
Raise our hands up on the same count.
Rap our bones against the closed door.
Then, just as suddenly, there's nothing.

Truly.

No more.

Walthamstow Wetlands

Passing shadow.
Like a pantomime of sorts.
Sorting through what life's supposed to be like.
Unpacking cardboard boxes;
water-stained, and broken wheels trailing.
Reflections on the water, paired by
tranquil clouds;
calling the rains down
greyly upon my eyes.
See hardly anything but
hard lines, and
wicked steel teeth.
Chain me and unchain me.
I am always free,
but maybe unaware of this
sometimes.

Just seems so easy to forget.

Estilos del Amor

Blue boxers pink underwear
and nothing
but heat against heat.
Arms and legs tangled
much defeating the purpose
of bedsheets.
Breath parts your lips
in the small space between
my neck and my cheek.
This is how you love me.

Pulses racing across the space
of at least two feet
at all times.
Too afraid to touch me.
Not knowing that I might want you to;
and in hindsight
first encounters are awkward.
Much too early
to read any warning signs
that a previous love may have left behind.

Rough hands wandering.
Gentle and skillful and curious still
even after all this time.
Thinking your fingers had found all the answers
they needed to know.
I feel your mouth coaxing against mine
pleading *quiero ver más de ti.*
I wonder with morbid curiosity
if the shape of this love is defined
by the total of all former heartbreaks combined.

In the space between
getting to know you
and knowing for sure

not unlike guilty hands
we are tied by a similar yearning.
A similar pleasure in learning
the ways we might care for each other.
Just the way tightly wound bodies
may shy at first touch,
so too may they unfold underneath the allure
of such sweet and seductive estilos del amor.

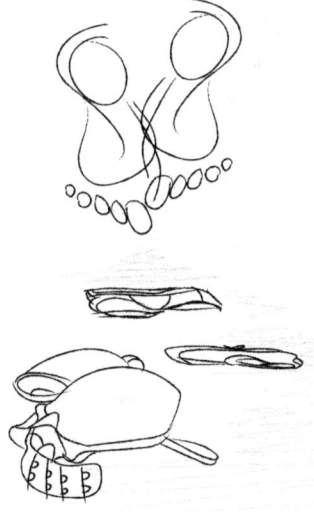

Dark Eyes

I can sleep warmly in
the crook of your smile.
Smiling more than I can admit
I have in quite a while.
Tender hook of your arms
above my waist, leaves
enough for me to breathe
softly, but slowly chased
by the wind, which
picks up small tendrils of your hair.
Curling around your temples.
The quiet nubs you call ears still fairly
accurate in their accounts
of my unintelligible mumblings.
Grumblings in the night.
Whisperings of "I love you's"
and tender caresses.
Tousled tresses
which fall into your dark eyes.
Flickering like tiny flames,
in the heart of the dark,
you are light.

The Fire, The Fight

Where did the jaws of you leave to?
Where was that supposed fight?
What to make me believe if not of
that impassioned, something fearsome bite
you claimed was yours,

but nothing more,

than tears and pitiful

wet pillow cheeks.

I lie, you see.

I do know where those jaws have went.
I do see where the fight first stepped.
Moved me to believe that inside of you
of course there lives that flame
and passion so bright.

Love could not contain ours,

but only dwindled down

to the fearsome almost nothing,

but never blew out.

Forever and still beating in us.

Neck Smell

It's the neck smell.
Grasping onto leaves.
Tree branch scrapes
and pricks
as accidental
and unmeaning as thorns.
"I love you," I think to myself.
Ball my hands into
the insides of your sweatshirt.
Nails gently caress the small river canals,
the sloping valley of your back.
It's just that neck smell and you.
Anchor of safety, arms around me.
Pull intently with those grounding quiet eyes.
Moon-faced you,
and that constellation-spotted skin.
You teach me how I want to be.
Child of everything.
Curious reinforcer of my theory.
Only thing I'm certain of
is my crippling uncertainty,
yet holding fast to little things, certainly.
Curtain of your lashes over me.
Like the reassuring pressure
of your fingers laced
between my crookedness.
Like the beat inside you
thumping softly in my ear.
More of this, please.

Hospital Bed Confessions

My bones have started clicking now.
Clickety-cracking
ancient typewriter keys,
and sometimes supper,
spindle-fisted tools.
Adept only at gripping
visco-licious
spoonfuls of red jello.
These are what
a healthy body
might call "fingers."

Hospital bed.
The now complete extension
of my lonely world.
Young pretty thing, "nurse" perches,
false-perky,
chirping in her corner chair.
Holding my tree trunk, tendonitis hands.
Warming them slightly from nostalgia's cold.
Gently trying to relate to me she cares.
Seems a sweet sentiment,
but, truthfully I don't.

Because it's you.
It's those sparse, yet-un-forgotten
memories of you,
that pull me closer to the bliss I'd hoped for.
Soon as you'd gone, that's when I decided
I was done.
Mind made itself stubbornly up,
the way minds do,
(the way mine does)
that the end of breathing was not nearly
as frightening to grapple with anymore.

'Cause I've lived long, and good and well,
and have you most of all to blame
for that fact, love.
Milky eyes, once brown, and once
so loving, cry now.
Can only scarcely make your face out
from behind these half-mast eyelids anymore.
Remember when we were kids
you smiled with those pretty lips,
soft and full and fitted well against mine?

Take me to where they've gone now.

AUTHOR'S NOTE

A great deal (most actually)
of these poems, were written
during prolonged periods of hurting,

growing,
mistaking,
and healing.

The darkest sentiments,
seem much farther past now.
Much smaller in the rearview.

The brighter ones,
I am only just beginning
to truly accustom my eyes to.

Creating,
impacting,
and loving,

are what the future is for
(and mine, in particular).
Here is to many more years of these.

ABOUT THE AUTHOR

Marjorie A. Thomas is an American poet, illustrator, musician, and filmmaker from the sunny suburban sprawls of Los Angeles, California. She resides currently in the San Francisco Bay Area, where she is pursuing dual degrees in Cinema and Psychology at San Francisco State University. When she is not scribbling one-liner poem ideas in her collection of a million notebooks, or tentatively dog-earring her precious book finds, she enjoys travelling, wandering the aisles of her local Trader Joe's, and hunting down that one magical café, in which there is no such problem as "writers block." *Roadmap Hands (and other reaching poems)* is her first collection of self-published work.